It Wasn't Me

By: Leah Orr & Alyssa Orr
Illustrated by: Josephine Lepore

First published by Dog Ear Publishing
4010 W. 86th Street, Ste H
Indianapolis, IN 46268
www.dogearpublishing.net

ISBN: 978-145750-698-7

Printed in the United States of America

Dedicated to everyone
who has ever been blamed for something they didn't do.

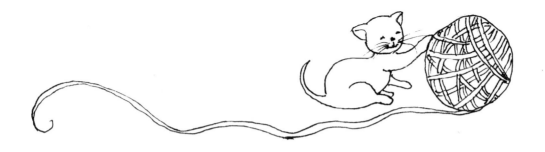

My family's house is filled with lots of kids and pets, but my mom always blames me for making a mess.

This past year I was blamed for big messes around the house you will see.

But I keep telling my mom...."It wasn't me!"

One snowy day in January, I put my snow boots by the door.

Mom said, "Peter, did you leave these snow prints all over my floor?"

I looked at my mom as she scowled at me.

And simply said... "It wasn't me."

In February I made Valentine's Day cards for school.

I made red hearts that were really cool.

I put them in my backpack, as mom stood and stared…..
At the glue and red paper stuck on the table and chair.

My mom shook her head and said, "Peter, I don't believe what I see."
Again I said… "It wasn't me."

In March, my brothers and I pretended we were Leprechauns searching for gold.

We searched under cushions, rugs, and pillows new and old.

One pillow exploded and feathers flew...

All over me and the family room too.

Mom ran into the room as my brothers fled.

Feathers flew everywhere, and stuck to my hands, feet, and head.

She screamed, "Clean this mess Peter, then go straight to bed."

I don't know how the feathers got free,

But, I said to my mom, "I promise...it wasn't me!"

During the months of April and May,

I helped my mom water the flowers after school every day.

Until one day when the hose got away.

I felt a tug on the hose; it flew out of my hand and I tripped on a pail.

The water hose soaked our neighbor, old lady Abigail.

Old lady Abigail was angry as can be….

I said, "I am so sorry……..But, It wasn't me."

The Summer months of June, July, and August were the most fun.

My brothers and I played in the pool in the hot summer sun.

After drying off, we played video games in the house.

My mom then noticed a very soaked couch.

She said, "Peter, the couch is ruined. I am so upset."

I told her…"It wasn't me, I dried off completely. I am not wet!"

September, October, and November are the months of Fall.

My brothers and I raked leaves in the yard into piles big and tall.

A giant gust of wind blew the leaves onto dad's car.

I had never seen leaves fly so fast and so far.

Mom asked, "Why is dad's car covered with leaves?"

I told her "It wasn't me… The leaves whipped through the air on a great big breeze."

In the middle of the night on Christmas Eve,

We heard a crash and woke up to see,

Lying on the floor was our Christmas Tree.

The cats were tangled in the lights,

The cage door was open and the birds were in flight,

My little brother was most upset, because….

The dog ate the cookies we made for Santa Claus.

But the best Christmas gift of all you see,

Was when mom finally realized, It wasn't me.

LEAH ORR, Best Selling Children's Author

Leah Orr resides in Weston, Florida with her husband and three daughters. Leah has written 4 books. *It Wasn't Me* is the most recent. *It Wasn't Me* is mostly enjoyed by Kindergarten, First and Second Graders.

Peter, The character in Leah's new book, continues to get blamed for making messes around the house, but he keeps telling his mom, " **It Wasn't Me**." Enjoy the mischief unfold as you turn the pages of this engaging whodunit mystery.

"This book is most exciting for me because it is written and illustrated by 3 generations of women in our family", said Leah Orr.

Leah donates a large portion of the profit from her books to the Cystic Fibrosis Foundation. Upon learning that her daughter Ashley was diagnosed with Cystic Fibrosis (while still in the womb), Orr knew she wanted to do something special. With some input from her mother and three daughters, it was decided that she'd write books to benefit the Cystic Fibrosis Foundation. The Orr family has raised more than $650,000 over the past 10 years for the CF Foundation.

Leah has recently been featured on ABC's Health Watch, NBC Today South Florida, CBS South Florida, CBS This Morning Virginia, NBC the 10! Show Philadelphia, Fox 4 News Morning Blend, National Syndicated, "The Daily Buzz", and Lifetime TV's "The Balancing Act." Leah has been featured in Publications such as: Forbes Magazine, Medical News Today, The Boston Globe, The Miami Herald, The Sun-Sentinel, etc. Ashley was also a recipient of Oprah's generosity in "The Big Give".

Orr grew up in Boston, MA and is a graduate of the University of Miami.

Other books by Leah Orr include Messy Tessy, Kyle's First Crush, and Kyle's First Playdate. More information is available at www.leahorr.com

Alyssa Orr

Alyssa Orr is the daughter of Leah Orr. She is an 8th grader at the Sagemont School in Weston, Florida. Alyssa recently attended a leadership program at Harvard University which motivated her to raise additional funds to help find a cure for her sister Ashley's disease. This is Aly's first children's book.

Josephine Lepore- Illustrator

Josephine Lepore is Leah Orr's mom and Alyssa Orr's grandmother. She teaches Art to children in an after-school program at the Nazzaro Center in the North End of Boston. Her students contribute generously every year in the fight against Cystic Fibrosis. Josephine donates a portion from the sale of her artwork to Cystic Fibrosis Research and has donated many of her works which are auctioned at CF Benefits both in Massachusetts and Florida.

Special Thanks to:

Ms. Villaverde's creative writing class at the Sagemont School
in Weston, Florida

Mrs. Russo and the Altavesta Elementary School
in Woburn, Massachusetts

Fabianna Diaz – Boca Advertising

My daughters, Aly, Camy & Ashley,
who continue to tell me each and every day….
Mom, It Wasn't Me!

Can you find the following hidden objects?

An alligator
A bird
A bunny
A butterfly
A ghost
An inchworm
A ladybug
A squirrel